ROBOTS

by bob staake

viking

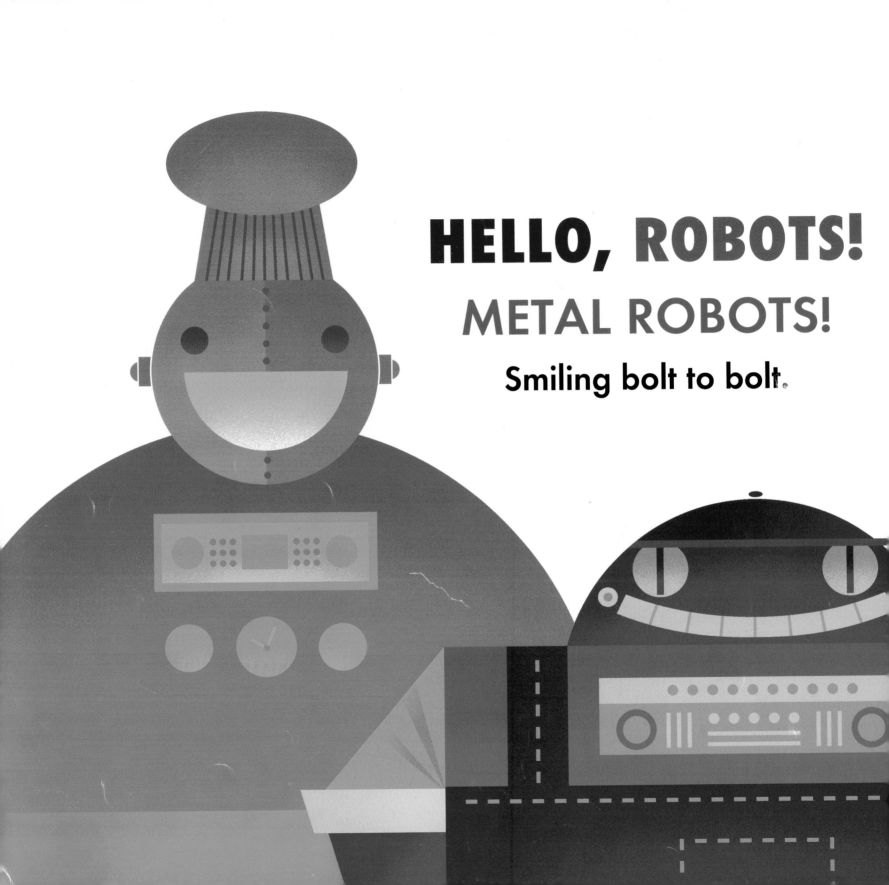

HELLO, ROBOTS!

METAL ROBOTS!

Smiling bolt to bolt.

BLINK's the one who cooks our meals.

ZINC can fix things made of steel.

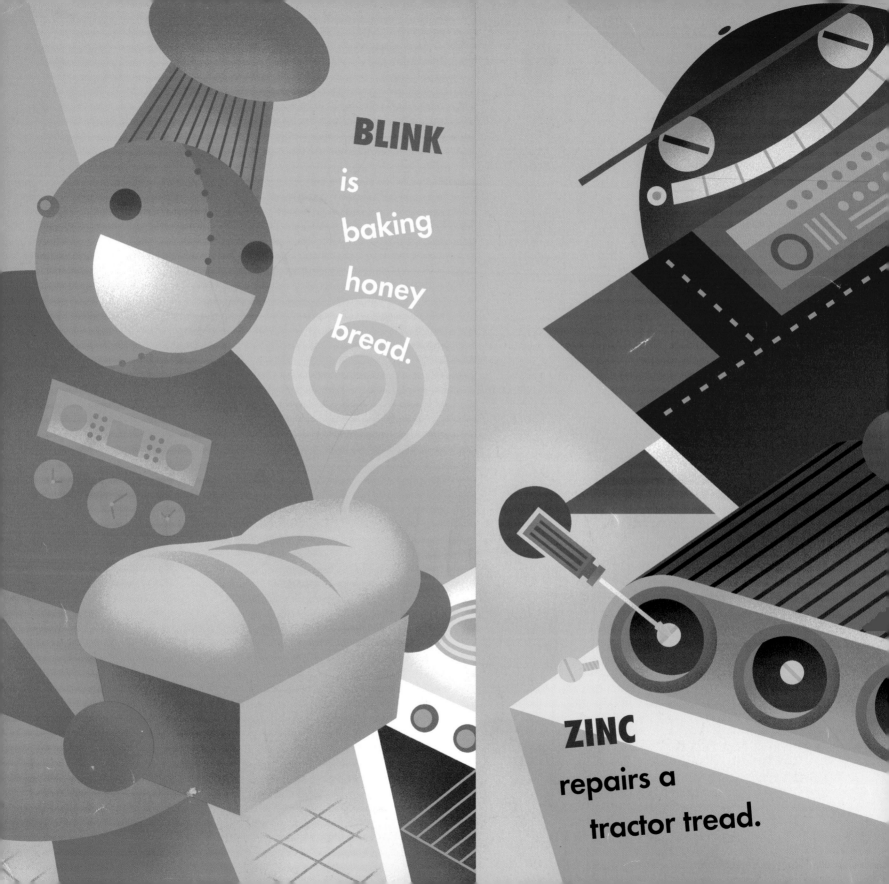

BLINK is baking honey bread.

ZINC repairs a tractor tread.

ZIP

mops

up

the

kitchen

floor.

BLIP,

he mows

the lawn

and more.

BLINK, he cooks a pot of stew.
ZINC repairs a clock or two.
BLIP, he plants a lemon tree.
ZIP dusts off the wood TV.

Hello, robots!
Metal robots!
Smiling bolt
to bolt!

Sunny skies and tea to sip.
Robots go outside
with **BLIP!**

Lots of backyard work to do.
A robot's job is never through!

BLINK, he bakes
an apple pie.

ZINC repairs a
birdhouse high.

BLIP, he rakes
a mound of grass.

ZIP shines up
the window glass.

Hello, robots!
Metal robots!
Smiling bolt to bolt!

Skies begin to darken gray.
Clouds block out the sunny day.

Plip plop,
plip plop!

Raindrops fall,
drenching robots one and all.

Rain gets in the robots four,
soaking buttons, lights, and more.

Clouds fly off
and who's amazed?

Four zapped
robots, looking
dazed!

BLINK, he **BAKES**
a birdhouse high.

ZINC REPAIRS
the apple pie.

BLIP, he RAKES
the window glass.

IP SHINES up a
ound of grass.

BLINK, he **COOKS** a clock or two.
ZINC REPAIRS a pot of stew.
BLIP, he PLANTS a wood TV.
ZIP DUSTS OFF a lemon tree.

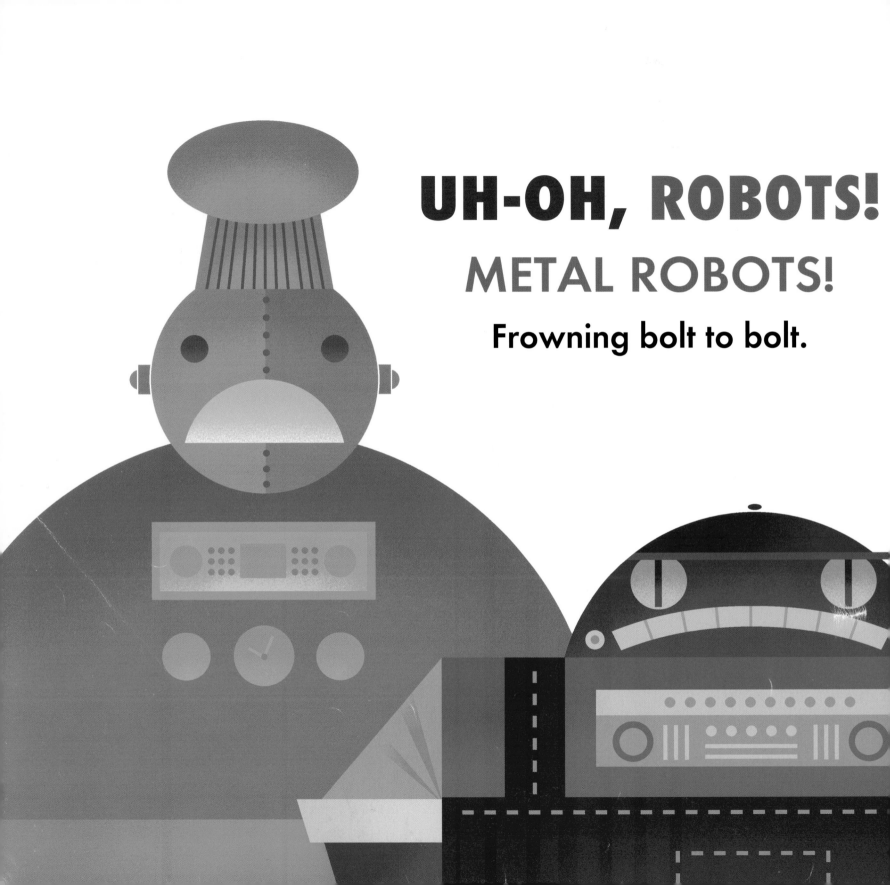

UH-OH, ROBOTS!

METAL ROBOTS!

Frowning bolt to bolt.

Something's wrong.
Something's quirky.
Robot brains don't
seem too perky.

Maybe if their
heads they switch,
that might fix their
awful glitch!

BLINK and ZINC
pop off their heads.
WARNING lights,
they flash bright red.

BLIP and **ZIP**,
they do it too,
swap their heads
in switcheroo.

Will the problem
now be fixed,
with the robot
heads all mixed?

BLINK cooks plump tomatoes ripe.

ZINC repairs leaky pipe

BLIP trims back a lilac bush.

ZIP, he dusts by sneezing—
swoosh!

BLINK wheel
out a chocolate tar
ZINC repair
the serving car

BLIP brings tulips in a pot.

ZIP cleans off a stubborn spot.

HELLO, ROBOTS!
METAL ROBOTS!
Smiling bolt to bolt.

To Jack

VIKING
Published by Penguin Group
Penguin Young Readers Group, 345 Hudson Street, New York, New York 10014, U.S.A.
Penguin Books Ltd, 80 Strand, London WC2R 0RL, England
Penguin Books Australia Ltd, 250 Camberwell Road, Camberwell, Victoria 3124, Australia
Penguin Books Canada Ltd, 10 Alcorn Avenue, Toronto, Ontario, Canada M4V 3B2
Penguin Books (N.Z.) Ltd, 182-190 Wairau Road, Auckland 10, New Zealand

First published in 2004 by Viking, a division of Penguin Young Readers Group

1 3 5 7 9 10 8 6 4 2

Copyright © Bob Staake, 2004

LIBRARY OF CONGRESS CATALOGING-IN-PUBLICATION DATA
Staake, Bob, date–
Hello, robots / by Bob Staake.
p. cm.
Summary: Nothing can stop hard-working robots, Blink, Zinc, Blip, and Zip,
from performing their many household tasks until they get caught in a downpour.
ISBN 0-670-05905-6 (hardcover)
[1. Robots—Fiction. 2. Humorous stories. 3. Stories in rhyme.] I. Title.
PZ8.3.S778He 2004
[E]—dc22
2004000494

Manufactured in China
Book design by Jim Hoover
Set in Futura EF Demi-Bold

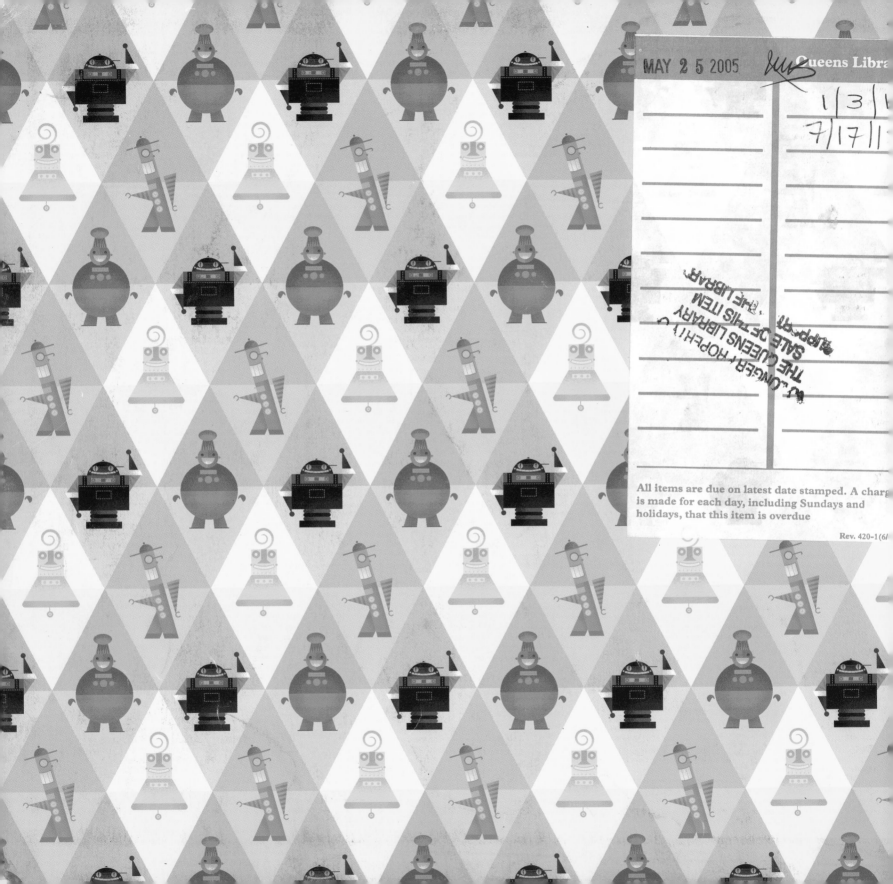